Most Valuable Player

STEVE YOUNG

Chris W. Sehnert

Published by Abdo & Daughters, 4940 Viking Drive, Suite 622, Edina, Minnesota 55435.

Printed in the United States.

Cover Photo credit: Allsport Photos
Interior Photo credits: Wide World Photos

Edited by Bob Italia

Library of Congress Cataloging-in-Publication Data

Sehnert, Chris W.
Steve Young / Chris W. Sehnert.
p. cm. -- (M.V.P.)
Includes index.

Summary: Traces the football career of the left-handed quarterback, from his days at Brigham Young University through his brief career with the USFL and the Tampa Bay Bucaneers to his sucess with the San Francisco Forty-Niners.

ISBN 1-56239-543-2
1. Young, Steve, 1961---Juvenile literature. 2. Football players--United States--biography--juvenile literature. 3. San Francisco 49ers (Football team)---juvenile literature. [1. Young, Steve, 1961-- . 2. Football players.] I. Title. II. Series: M.V.P., most valuable players.

GV939.Y69S48 1996
796.332'092--dc20 95-44799
[B] CIP
AC

Contents

THE BEST IN THE BUSINESS

Steve Young is a quarterback at the top of his profession. He has won the National Football League's (NFL's) passing title four straight seasons. He has led his team to a Super Bowl championship, and has been the NFL's Most Valuable Player two times. He has worked hard to reach the top.

To be a leader. To never give up. To stay focused when everything is going against you. These are qualities National Football League scouts look for when choosing a quarterback for their team. Steve Young of the San Francisco 49ers has all these skills—and more.

ROOTS

Jon Steven Young was born October 11, 1961, in Salt Lake City, Utah. When he was eight years old his family moved to Greenwich, Connecticut. Steve was the oldest of five children. He has three brothers and a sister. His mother's name is Sherry.

Steve Young is a quarterback at the top of his profession.

Throughout his life, Steve has lived in the shadows of great men. His father, LeGrande Young, is a corporate lawyer in New York. LeGrande played football for Brigham Young University. LeGrande was given the nickname "Grit" at a young age, and it characterizes his personality.

Steve's family belongs to the Church of Jesus Christ of Latter Day Saints. Members of this church are called Mormons. Mormon's do not smoke cigarettes or drink alcohol.

Brigham Young was Steve's great-great-great grandfather. He was the second president of the Mormon Church. In 1847, Brigham led his Mormon followers across the plains of the Midwestern United States to settle near the Great Salt Lake in Utah. He became Utah's first territorial governor, and the namesake of Brigham Young University (BYU).

YOUNGER DAYS

As a boy growing up in Greenwich, Steve played sports to make friends with the older kids in the neighborhood. When he was nine years old, he played quarterback in a Pop Warner football league. His boyhood hero was Roger Staubach of the Dallas Cowboys.

Steve attended Greenwich High School. As a sophomore, his hands were hardly big enough to grip the football. He played for the junior varsity squad that year. In one game, six of his ten passes were intercepted.

Steve did not give up. He set a simple goal for himself. He would try to improve a little bit each day. By his senior year, he was captain of the football team, the baseball team and the basketball team!

Steve's great speed made him successful on the high school football field. The Greenwich offense used the wishbone formation, an offensive scheme where two tailbacks are spread out behind the quarterback in a wishbone shape.

The most common play out of the wishbone is the quarterback option. In this play, the quarterback takes the hike and rolls towards the sidelines before cutting up field. The quarterback has the option to throw the ball up field, pitch the ball back to a following tailback, or put his head down and smash through the line. This is where Steve developed his hard-nosed running style.

A YOUNG COUGAR

Steve's family background, his excellent school work, and athletic ability led him to Brigham Young University in 1980. The first year of college was another tough test for the young, left-handed quarterback.

The BYU Cougars traditionally play a passing style offense. Steve was recruited for his running ability. For this reason, head coach LaVell Edwards wanted to move him to the defensive backfield. Steve practiced the safety position and continued to work on his passing skills.

Steve was the eighth string quarterback. Jim McMahon was number one. In 1981, McMahon would finish his BYU career as one of the highest ranked quarterbacks in college football history. Later, he would join the NFL, and lead the Chicago Bears to a victory in Super Bowl XX.

Brigham Young quarterback, Jim McMahon.

While McMahon set passing records for the Cougars, Steve stumbled on the practice squad.

He became so frustrated after only a few weeks he wanted to quit and go back to Connecticut. His father told Steve, "You can quit, but you can't come home." Steve finished his freshman year as the junior varsity quarterback.

WHAT A FIND

Steve steadily improved his passing skills in his first year. However, had it not been for quarterback coach Ted Tollner, he may have become a defensive back.

In January 1980, Steve was working out with some other quarterbacks in BYU's field house. Tollner jogged by, and stopped to watch. What he saw was an eighteen-year-old lefty with a lot of athletic ability and a very quick throwing release.

Tollner talked to head coach LaVell Edwards about what he had seen that day. Edwards agreed to keep Steve at quarterback. When the 1981 season started, Steve was the backup quarterback behind McMahon. Steve spent his sophomore season on the sidelines studying McMahon's every move.

MY TURN

McMahon headed for the pros after the 1981 season. He had left a legacy at BYU, having gained more yards passing than any quarterback in college football history.

In 1982, Steve's junior season, he became the Cougars' starting quarterback. He had worked hard for it. In a single practice, he would often throw the ball 200 times. He had developed pinpoint accuracy.

In a 51-3 victory over the University of Texas at El Paso, Steve passed for 399 yards. In the same game, he ran for 97 yards! He finished the season passing for 3,100 yards and rushing for 407 yards. His combined production that season still ranks among the highest in NCAA history.

Steve's senior season was even better. In 1983, he broke McMahon's single-season record for average

Steve Young passing for Brigham Young University.

Steve Young responds to BYU fans with a number one.

yards per game. He passed for 3,902 yards while running for 444 yards. His average of 395.1 yards per game was an NCAA record that stood for six years.

The Cougars won 11 of 12 games that season, and earned a trip to the Holiday Bowl where they beat Missouri. At season's end, they were ranked number eight in college football.

Off the field, Steve was finishing a double major in finance and international relations ahead of schedule! Because of his high marks, he was named one of the National Football Foundation and Hall of Fame's Scholar-Athletes.

Steve was an NCAA All-American quarterback for 1983. He finished second in the Heisman Trophy voting for the nation's top college football player. He had come a long way from the stumbling freshman of 1980. Now he wanted a professional football career, and a law degree.

L.A. EXPRESS

After two years of good fortune, Steve's road to success would again turn bumpy. The year 1984 turned out to be strange for a top NFL draft candidate.

That year, the Cincinnati Bengals owned the first pick in the NFL draft. Bengal's management wanted to sign Steve. Before drafting him, they offered him a guaranteed four-year, four-million dollar contract. Steve's choices were complicated, however.

A new professional football league, the United States Football League (USFL), had started in 1983. The USFL played its games in spring instead of autumn. The USFL team owners were among the richest people in the world. They offered college stars huge sums of money hoping their league could be as good as the NFL.

The Los Angeles Express was one of the new USFL teams. The team's owner was William Oldenburg, the wealthy founder of an international investment company. He negotiated with Steve's father and agent, Leigh Steinberg, on a contract that would make Steve the highest paid player in professional sports history.

Steve was not too excited about the money. He did want to play, however. The Express offered him the chance to be a starting quarterback. In the NFL, he could spend years as a backup before getting a chance to play. Dallas Cowboy's quarterback Roger Staubach called Steve and urged him not to go to the USFL. Taking his father's advice, however, Steve eventually signed with the L.A. Express.

EXPRESS TO NOWHERE

Steve was suddenly a rich man, but the money made him uncomfortable. He lived his life as though nothing had changed. He continued to drive his father's 1965

Steve Young stands with L.A. Express owner, J. William Oldenburg.

Oldsmobile, and shared an apartment with six of his new teammates.

He played two seasons with the Express, but the new league was crumbling. Oldenburg lost his entire fortune before Steve's second season in 1985. The team was kicked out of their training camp headquarters because management had not paid the rent.

Other owners in the league chipped in to pay player salaries, but the team was left without a practice field. On the way to the final game of the year, the bus driver pulled over and refused to continue unless he was paid. Steve passed the hat, and played his last game for the USFL. The league folded before the 1986 season, but Steve had already moved on.

THE LOWLY BUCS

The next stepping stone for Steve was with the Tampa Bay Buccaneers. Seeing the USFL was likely to go

Steve Young with the L.A. Express, being chased by an Oakland Invader defenseman.

under, the Buccaneers drafted Steve in the summer of 1984. Steve paid his way out of his USFL contract, and signed a six-year deal with Tampa in 1985.

The next two seasons were only slightly better than the previous two. Steve was finally an NFL quarterback, but he played on one of the worst teams in its history. The Buccaneers won 4 games and lost 28 in 1985 and '86. The offensive line was so poor at protecting the quarterback, one of Steve's coaches warned him to be careful.

In two seasons with Tampa, Steve threw 11 touchdowns and 21 interceptions. Nearly half of the passes he threw fell incomplete. Veteran NFL quarterback Steve DeBerg was Steve's teammate. DeBerg told Steve to go to a team with good coaches. He suggested the San Francisco 49ers.

WALSH'S WONDERS

The head coach of the 49ers in 1986 was Bill Walsh. He had developed a new style of offense in San Francisco which featured the passing attack. His team had already won two Super Bowls in the 1980s, led by Joe Montana.

Sid Gillman was the 49ers passing coach. He had developed an explosive passing attack in the 1960s as head coach of the San Diego Chargers. He had also been Steve's quarterback coach with the Express. He talked to Walsh about Steve.

"Sid Gillman was telling me this was the finest quarterback athlete he'd ever seen," Walsh told Peter King in a *Sports Illustrated* interview. "Tampa couldn't protect the passer, plus they were running a dated offense. So Steve looked bad there. What scouts saw when they watched Steve with Tampa was a left-handed, inaccurate quarterback; it fulfilled their old wives' tale about how left-handed quarterbacks couldn't be good in the NFL. I set about a quiet campaign to get him."
In April 1987, Steve was traded to San Francisco.

THE UNDERSTUDY

Steve had joined a winning team, but at what price? He certainly could not expect to start with a healthy Joe Montana on the roster.

He had been an understudy before. Watching Jim McMahon in college taught Steve how to be a drop back passer. Now, he would study a two-time Super Bowl MVP.

Steve didn't play much over the next four seasons. Bill Walsh left the team in 1989. Defensive coordinator George Seifert replaced him. As Steve stood on the sidelines, Montana led the 49ers to victories in Super Bowl XXIII (January 1989) and Super Bowl XXIV (January 1990).

The 1989 season was, perhaps, Montana's finest ever. His 112.4 passing rating was the highest in NFL history. He had given San Francisco back-to-back Super Bowl titles and four championships in eight years! His popularity was soaring.

It looked as if Steve would never get his chance to lead this team. Even if he did, how could he ever measure up to Joe? When he did play, fans criticized him while comparing him to Montana.

WHAT A BACKUP

Steve got his chance to be the leader in 1991. Montana went down with a torn elbow tendon during the preseason.

Steve started ten games for the 49ers in 1991. He injured his knee in the ninth game and was forced back to the bench. This time, he watched third-string quarterback Steve Bono lead the team.

Later, he would point to those days as a turning point in his career. "I used to try to do everything possible all at once, sometimes on every play," Steve said. "After I got hurt, I realized it was my job to orchestrate the offense, not play every instrument."

Steve returned for the final game of the 1991 season, a 52-14 win over the Chicago Bears. He completed 21 of his 32 passes for 338 yards and 3 touchdowns. He ran the ball for 63 yards and scored another touchdown.

Steve finished the 1991 season as the highest ranked passer in the NFL. He threw 17 touchdowns and was intercepted only 8 times. His NFL passing rating was 101.8, the highest since Montana's 1989 season.

The 49ers 10-6 record was not enough to reach the playoffs, however. Once again, Montana fans put the blame on Steve.

TAKE THAT!

Montana was not ready to return when the 1992 season began. Steve was anxious to improve on 1991.

He did just that! Steve commanded the best offense in the league in 1992. The 49ers averaged 387.2 yards and 26.9 points per game. They had the NFL's best record at 14-2.

Steve finished the season with a 107.0 passing rating which led the league. It was the first time in NFL history a quarterback had a rating over 100 two years in a row!

It was the Dallas Cowboys' year, however. They ended the 49ers great season with a 30-20 victory in the NFC Championship game. The Cowboys went on to beat the Buffalo Bills in Super Bowl XXVII.

After the season, Steve's teammates gave him the Len Eshmont award for "inspirational and courageous play." He was voted the NFL's Most Valuable Player.

NOW WHAT?

The 49ers' management had an interesting decision to make after the 1992 season. Joe Montana was healthy again. He had returned to standing ovations in the 1992 final regular-season game. Meanwhile, their "second-stringer" was now considered the best quarterback in football.

Steve commanded the best offense in the league in 1992.

Every 49er fan had an opinion. Steve had been the best passer in the game for the past two seasons. Joe had led the team to four Super Bowl titles. How could both players stay on the same team?

The answer was simple: they could not. Montana began looking for another team. The Kansas City Chiefs needed veteran leadership. Joe was the right man for the job.

Steve earned his law degree at BYU during the off-season. When he returned to San Francisco, he was alone as king in the 49ers' court!

CHANGE THAT TUNE

The 1993 NFL season was similar to the 1992 season in many ways. The Dallas Cowboys defeated the 49ers in the NFC Championship, then defeated Buffalo in the Super Bowl.

The league's leading passer was also a repeat performer. Steve dominated nearly every quarterback category in 1993. His 29 touchdown passes led the league for the second straight year. His 101.5 passing rating made him the first quarterback to ever win the passing title three straight years.

Steve had won the NFL's MVP award in 1992. He was the best quarterback in football. There was just one goal Steve Young had yet to accomplish.

XXIX

1994 was a very good year. The San Francisco 49ers were back on top. Their 13-3 record was the best in the NFL.

Steve led all quarterbacks with 35 touchdown passes. He threw 324 completions for 3,969 yards. He scored seven more touchdowns carrying the ball himself. His NFL 112.8 passing rating eclipsed Joe Montana's mark as the highest in the history of the game. The league's MVP award was his again. He had become the best passer in the NFL for the fourth straight time!

The playoffs began the way they had the past two seasons. The Dallas Cowboys met the San Francisco 49ers in the NFC title game.

This time the 49ers came out on top. Capitalizing on Dallas turnovers, San Francisco took a 21-0 lead less than eight minutes into the game. The Cowboys had won the last two Super Bowls. This time they couldn't overcome their early mistakes.

Steve threw touchdown passes to running back Ricky Watters and wide receiver Jerry Rice. He scored the last touchdown himself on a 3-yard run. The 49ers dethroned Dallas with a 38-28 win. They would meet the San Diego Chargers in Super Bowl XXIX.

RECORD DAY

Steve would finally get his chance to lead his team to an NFL championship. He had gained all the experience he would ever need for this day. On Super Sunday, he was ready.

The game was played at Joe Robbie Stadium in Miami, Florida. The 49ers called the coin toss, received the opening kickoff, and the rest was history.

San Francisco set the record for the fastest opening touchdown drive in Super Bowl history. On the fourth play of the game, Steve threw a 44-yard touchdown pass to Jerry Rice. Only 1:24 into the game, the 49ers were up 7-0.

Next, they set a Super Bowl record for scoring touchdowns on their first three offensive possessions. By halftime, San Francisco led the Chargers 28-10. Steve had already thrown four touchdown passes.

The 49ers continued their domination in the second half. Steve threw a fifth touchdown pass to tie a Super Bowl record held by Joe Montana.

One minute into the fourth quarter, he found Jerry Rice in the end-zone again. It was Rice's third touchdown of the day, and a record-breaking sixth touchdown pass for Steve Young.

The San Francisco 49ers became the first team to win five Super Bowl titles. They beat the San Diego Chargers 49-26.

Steve finished the day with 24 completions in 36 attempts for 325 yards. He threw six touchdown passes, and no interceptions. He was named the MVP of Super Bowl XXIX.

OUT OF THE SHADOWS

Steve Young has lived much of his life in the shadows of great men. He has risen above his struggles to become one of the great players in football history. "Everything that happened was just what I needed," he said. "In a way I think we all have that in life-tough experiences and things that make us better people."

Steve hasn't always been on top. He has taken criticism and learned from those who came before him. He has built on daily successes to become the very best at what he does.

He also continues to develop his life outside of football. He has a graduate degree in Law from BYU, and he plans to take the California bar exam soon.

Steve has a healthy way of dealing with the success his hard work has brought him. He contributes his time and money to many organizations. He has done extensive charitable work with Native Americans as well as a family of Russian immigrants. He donates money to support sports programs for kids in his community. He continues to demonstrate what it takes to be an MVP.

Steve Young, most valuable player.

STEVE YOUNG'S ADDRESS

You can write to Steve Young at the following address:

Steve Young
c/o San Francisco 49ers
4949 Centennial Blvd.
Santa Clara, CA 95054

If you want a response, please enclose a self-addressed, stamped envelope.

Glossary

AFC: The American Football Conference. One of two conferences in the NFL.

All-American: A person chosen as the best amateur athlete at their position.

Bar Exam: A test taken by college graduates allowing them to practice their profession.

Brigham Young University: A center of higher education in the state of Utah.

Contract: A written agreement a player signs when they are hired by a professional team.

Corporate Lawyer: A professional legal representative who advises businesses.

Draft: A system in which new players are distributed to professional sports teams.

End-Zone: The area at either end of the playing field between the goal line and the end line.

Field House: A building on a college campus which allows field sports to be practiced indoors.

Finance: The science of the management of money and other assets.

Heisman Trophy: An award presented each year to the most outstanding college football player.

Interception: A pass in football which is caught by the opposition.

International Relations: The science of mutual dealings among persons of separate nations.

National Football League: The premier association of professional football teams, consisting of the American and National Football Conferences.

NCAA: An organization which oversees the administration of college athletics.

NFC: The National Football Conference. One of two conferences in the NFL.

Passing Rating: A system used in the NFL to measure a quarterback's efficiency passing the football.

Pop Warner Football: An organization of football teams for kids nine to twelve years old.

Scholar-Athletes: An award given to collegians who excel in both athletics and classroom studies.

Scout: One who is employed to observe and report on the strategies and players of other teams.

Super Bowl: The championship of the NFL, played between the American and National Conference champions.

Touchdown: An act of carrying, receiving, or gaining possession of the ball across the opponent's goal line for a score of six points.

Understudy: To be engaged in studying a role so as to be able to replace the regular performer when required.

Varsity: The principal team representing a university, college, or school in sports, games, or other competitions.

Veteran: A player with more than one year of professional experience.

Index